We've Got Twuddle Fairies

John Elford

Written for my family with a whole load of inspiration from the arrival of my first grand-daughter Lily.

Special thanks to Bill and Bob, without them this would not be possible.

WE1COME TO

WE'VE GOT
TWUDDLE FAIRIES

We've got Twuddle Fairies, they're all sorts of trouble.

They cause lots of mayhem and put things in a muddle.

When I put stuff away safe in a drawer

They mess it right up, and chuck some on the floor.

I put away gadgets as neat as I can

Not knowing these fairies have a mean plan.

They get inside and twuddle stuff up,

I once found my gloves in an upside-down cup.

It started with small things, in a place you will know,
The drawer in the kitchen where bits and bobs go.

I suspected some mischief cause I'm always so neat
But the drawer was a mess, and I thought I saw feet.

I've learned that they're clever, and quite hard to spot,

And I think that I've seen them, but most probably not,

They twiddle and twuddle right under my nose,

They get in my wardrobe and hide in my clothes.

TWUDDLE FAIRIES

TWUDDLE
FAIRIES

I know they are real and not just in fables

And I'm sure its **not** me who tangles my cables.

I'm a neat sort of person who likes stuff to be straight,

I even make sure that I close our front gate.

When a drawer in our house has just been shut
The fairies start working, it's fun for them but -

For a person like me who
wants things in order,

It muddles my brain - I can't
handle disorder.

TWUDDLE
FAIRIES

I went to the shed and I put things away
So that they're easy to find the very next day.

But when I went back, "oh what a fright!",
Those fairies had been and "oh what a sight"!

My wires were all crossed and my string was all tangled

My shed was a mess and the insides look mangled.

'That is NOT how I left it', I said to my buddy,

Even my boots, that were clean, are now muddy.

My dog sometimes jumps up in the midst of a dream
And he barks so loud that I let out a scream.
See I know he hears fairies, and I know he can tell
that a fairy is near, he can tell by the smell.

It's not just my drawers that they plague with their habit.

My school bags aren't safe, and if they can help it

They sneak inside and cause all sorts of tangles,

My best piece of string was tied up with my bangles.

And my teacher won't have it when my homework goes missing.

"It's the fairies" I say, but she just doesn't listen.

"They've done it again", but I've lost her attention

As she hands me a slip for another detention.

Now twuddling, I've learned, is not all that they do,
Oh no, they like laundry and hide in there too.
I hope this isn't too much of a shock,
But Twuddlers are known to run off with a sock.

Or talking of laundry here's a thing that they try
And mothers all over will let out a cry,
Just before mum puts the clothes in the wash,
They'll put a sweet in your pocket, I know - "oh gosh"!

They might even twuddle the temperature gauge.
It's enough to send people into a big rage.
They think it looks pretty when dark colours run,
They enjoy what they're doing, and think it is fun.

I thought they were trouble and I wanted them out

So I set up some cameras, I hid one in a sprout.

I put them around to see what they do,

I was very surprised, just like you will be too.

TWUDDLE
FAIRIES

You see I thought Twuddle Fairies were bad.

But I'll tell you some news, and I think you'll be glad.

I found out that they love the place they reside

They looked after my home with ferocious pride.

Home Sweet Home

I saw them once sat around playing Ludo.

The next time I looked
they were practicing Judo.

If anything came in our house
overnight,

The fairies would put up one heck of
a fight.

They keep our house clean and safe from small bugs,
And I saw them, at times, take on some big thugs,
Like monsters and bears and even baboons.
They hit burglars knees with really hard spoons.

I saw them hunt spiders and things that came in.

They woke me some nights with a terrible din

Having races across our big kitchen floor

On the backs of these beasts, then out the back door.

Some other things that were quite a surprise,

Twuddle Fairies can change, and choose their own size.

Sometimes they're big and sometimes their small

And sometimes they fade, I can't see them at all.

They may have wings, when they fly in the day

But night time I think, they can fold them away.

They use magic I'm sure, to do these great things.

"Who would have thought they have fold away wings"?

I'm happy I've seen the good that they do
They look after us folks, but they're naughty too.
An example of this, and they do it with ease
When dad turns his back, they hide his car keys.

TWUDDLE
FAIRIES

And   one   final   thing……………..

If mum wakes up with her hair all a mess,

A 'bad hair night' that fills her with stress,

I know that the fairies were at work in her hair,
They think it looks better, they really do care.

THANK YOU
FOR
READING

About the Author

Hi folks, I hope this book finds you well. I was persuaded by my children to write and illustrate this book. I usually write very serious ones about recovery from addiction, but as you can guess with two young children on the case with comments like "Dad, your books are soooo boring" I was spurred on to tackle the Twuddle Fairies.

We often make up bedtime stories and talk about Twuddle Fairies, (and Skully Adventures and Pebble Pixies) so here we are. I hope you enjoy the book.

There is a page at the back of the book that gives a quick overview of how I put this all together using (some, not all) pictures of our hotel, Somerton Lodge, and then applying various bits of software to make the magic happen.

I'd like to show a little of how I developed the illustrations for this book. Not being an arty person drawing any of these myself was a non runner, no way could I apply pen / paint to paper and produce anything that you would find recognisable. I've had some good inspiration from great people like Debby Crouch (Creative Wellness Journey) who uses art to help people focus on getting well from various illnesses.

What I found that I could do was use various bits of computer software to create the pictures. Some pictures are taken in our hotel and then converted into the various formats that made the finished pictures. I'm sure that if I can do it then so can you.

So here is a brief picture journey from start to finish.

1. This is the original picture of our hotel lounge taken with an iPhone.

2. I then did a bit of colouring using an app called Sketches.

3. Converting the pictures to art took a piece of software called Pastello (Pro).

4. Next came various picture downloads from Shutterstock.com or 123rf.com. These fairies for instance.

5. To cut them out so that I can put them into the pictures lead me to using a website called ClippingMagic.com

6. Using an apple computer and their standard word processing software (Pages) I pulled it all together to make the finished pictures and the complete book.

7. Self publishing through Amazon KDP took a bit of thinking as book size formatting was a bit tricky. A bit of advice use their templates from the very beginning.

Having previous experience made this process a whole lot easier.

So here's thanks to the modern world and the software and websites that made this book possible.

https://www.shutterstock.com

https://www.123rf.com

https://clippingmagic.com

https://tayasui.com/sketches/

https://jixipix.com/pastello/info-app-store.html

https://kdp.amazon.com

https://www.rhymezone.com

Printed in Great Britain
by Amazon

11620041R00016